My Treasury of
BEDTIME
TALES

hinkler

This book belongs to

· ·

My Treasury of BEDTIME TALES

Published by Hinkler Books Pty Ltd
45–55 Fairchild Street
Heatherton Victoria 3202 Australia
www.hinkler.com

hinkler

© Hinkler Books Pty Ltd 2008, 2015, 2017

Editor: Louise Coulthard
Art director: Paul Scott
Cover illustration: Manuel Šumberac
Internal design: Trudi Webb
Illustrators: Melissa Webb, Anton Petrov, Omar Aranda,
Suzie Byrne, Mirela Tufan and Dean Jones
Designers: Diana Vlad, Susanna Murray and Paul Scott
Prepress: Graphic Print Group

ISBN 978 1 4889 0915 3

Printed and bound in China

CONTENTS

INTRODUCTION

Fairytales have been told to children for centuries, engaging the imagination and opening up worlds of wonder and mystery. These tales have been popular through all the world's cultures and are an important inheritance of a rich oral folktale history that has developed throughout the ages. Over the years, scholars have found many ways to study and classify fairytales, with similar themes appearing in stories from cultures world-wide.

The Brothers Grimm are two of the earliest and best known collectors and scholars of the fairytale genre. The two brothers were born in Germany in the late 1700s and built their fairytale collection, *Children's and Household Tales*, throughout their lives. The final edition eventually contained over 200 stories.

Others have also contributed to the record of the fairytales we know and love today, with fairytale collections becoming increasingly popular for both adults and children. Hans Christian Andersen is one of the few writers to actually create new fairytales. He was born in Denmark in 1805 and his stories have become as beloved as the traditional tales recorded by the Grimms.

Sharing fairytales with children at bedtime is a wonderful way to build a love for this rich history, as well as connecting us with our past and those who shared these stories before us. These tales are bound to become favourites and you will find that they form part of your history too.

PUSS IN BOOTS

Once upon a time, there was an old miller who died, leaving nothing for his three sons apart from his mill, his donkey and his cat.

The three sons decided to split this poor property between themselves. The eldest son took the mill, the second son took the donkey and the youngest son received nothing but the cat.

Understandably, the youngest son was quite disappointed that his share was so poor. 'My brothers may make a handsome enough living if they combine their shares together,' said the youngest son, 'but, for my part, once I have eaten this cat and made a hat of his skin, I must die of hunger.'

The cat heard the youngest son saying all this, but he appeared to take no notice of it. Instead, he turned to his master with a grave and serious air and said, 'Do not worry yourself so, my master. All you have to do is give me a bag and get a pair of boots made for me so I may scamper easily through the thorns and brambles, and you shall soon see that, as my owner, you don't have such a poor share after all.'

Although the youngest son did not entirely trust what the cat had said, he remembered that he'd seen the cat play cunning tricks to catch rats and mice. The cat had hung himself by the heels to make the mice think he was dead and had hidden himself in the corn, so the cat's master did not completely despair of the cat helping him out of his situation.

Once his young master had given him his new boots and bag, the cat was very pleased. He thought he looked very gallant and elegant in his shiny boots. Wearing his new boots, the cat hung his bag around his neck and held its strings in his two forepaws. He went out into the fields and found some tender, juicy grass to put in the bag.

Then the cat went to a nearby rabbit warren where he knew a great number of rabbits lived. He stretched himself out on the ground as though he were dead, making sure that some of the grass in the bag was poking out. The cat lay there, waiting for some young rabbits, not yet acquainted with the tricks of the world, to come along and be tempted by the food in his bag.

The cat had barely lain himself down when a young and foolish rabbit hopped up. It sniffed at him, and then climbed into the bag to eat the tender grass. At once, the cat drew closed the strings, catching the rabbit unawares.

Proud of his catch, the cat headed off to the palace and asked to see the king. He was shown to the king's court, where he made a low bow to those assembled there.

'I have brought you, Sire, a rabbit from the warren of my noble lord and master, the Marquis of Carabas (which was the title that the cat was pleased to invent for his master),' said the cat. 'He commanded me to bring this to Your Majesty as a gift.'

The king was very pleased with the gift, as he was extremely fond of tasty rabbit.

'Tell thy master,' said the king, 'that I thank him and that I am well pleased with his gift.'

The cat departed, happy with the outcome of his endeavour.

Shortly after this, the cat hid himself amongst some tall corn in a field, again with his bag around his neck. He stood as still as a statue near the tastiest looking corn he could find and held his bag open. It wasn't long before two partridges came along and, in their efforts to eat the corn, fell into the open bag. At once, the cat drew the strings closed, catching both birds.

As he had done with the rabbit, the cat went to the palace and made a present of the partridges to the king. In the same way, the king received the partridges with great pleasure. The king even commanded his servants to reward the cat with a gold coin.

Over the course of the next two or three months, the cat continued to take some of his master's game as a gift to the king. The king was always very pleased to receive these offerings and he rewarded the cat with a gold coin.

One day, the cat discovered that the king was to go for a drive along the riverside to get some fresh air and enjoy the sunshine. The cat also discovered that the king was taking his daughter, the most beautiful princess in the world, with him on the drive.

The cat went to his master and said, 'If you will follow my advice, your fortune is made. You don't have to do anything apart from going to the river and having a bath at the spot that I show you. Just leave all the rest to me.'

The cat's master was confused as to why the cat was asking him to do this, but he did as the cat advised. While he was bathing, the king's carriage passed by.

At once, the cat cried out at the top of his voice, 'Help! Help! My master, the Marquis of Carabas, is drowning! Help! Help!'

Hearing the noise, the king looked out of the carriage window. Seeing the cat who had brought him so many gifts of game, he commanded his guards to immediately run to the assistance of his Lordship, the Marquis of Carabas.

As the king's guards were pulling the marquis out of the river, the cat hid his master's clothes under a large, heavy rock. Then the cat went up the coach and told the king that while his master was bathing, some thieves had come and stolen his clothes, even though the cat had cried out, 'Thieves! Thieves!' as loudly as he could. At once, the king commanded some guards to run and fetch one of his best suits for the Marquis of Carabas to wear.

The king was exceedingly polite to the marquis once he had put on the fine suit, as the clothes set off his good looks (for he was very handsome) and the king saw that his lovely daughter was very taken with the marquis. The marquis had only to exchange two or three respectful and tender glances with her before they found themselves in love. The king invited the marquis to join them on their drive.

The cat was overjoyed to see his plan succeeding. He marched on ahead of the coach and met some people mowing in a meadow, which was owned by a cruel ogre.

'Good mowers,' said the cat, 'the ogre who owns this field has asked me to tell you that if you do not tell the king that the meadow you are mowing belongs to the Marquis of Carabas, he will chop you up into tiny pieces and cook you in his pot!'

The mowers were very frightened of the ogre, so when the king drove past and asked them who owned the meadow, they all immediately answered, 'The Marquis of Carabas does, Your Majesty.'

'You have a fine meadow there,' the king said to the marquis.

'Yes Sire,' replied the marquis, thinking quickly. 'It gives me a good harvest every year.'

The cat continued on ahead, until he met with some reapers, who were harvesting corn in another field owned by the ogre.

'Good reapers,' said the cat, 'the ogre who owns this field has asked me to tell you that if you do not tell the king that this corn belongs to the Marquis of Carabas, he will chop you up into tiny pieces and cook you in his pot!'

And when the king passed the field in his carriage and asked them who owned it, they all replied, 'The Marquis of Carabas owns this corn, Your Majesty.'

The cat went on ahead again and told everyone he met that the ogre said to tell the King that the land was owned by the Marquis of Carabas. Everyone was so scared of the ogre that they did.

Eventually the cat came to the ogre's home, which was an enormous, stately castle. The ogre was the richest ogre ever known. The cat, who had discovered the ogre's magical talent, asked to see him, saying he couldn't pass by without paying his respects. After some grumbling, the ogre let him in and made him sit down.

'I have been told that you have an amazing gift,' said the cat to the ogre. 'They tell me that you can change yourself into any creature you choose, such as a lion. Surely this is not true?'

'It is true! If you don't believe me, let me prove it to you,' said the proud ogre, and he turned himself into a fierce, snarling lion.

The cat seemed so terrified at the sight of the lion that he jumped up and tried to climb on to a cupboard, which was rather awkward because of his boots. When he saw the ogre had finally returned to his normal form, he slowly climbed down.

'That is impressive!' said the cat. 'But I have also been told that you can take on the shape of the smallest animal, such as a mouse. Surely, though, that is impossible.'

'Impossible?' roared the ogre. 'Watch and you shall see!'

And the ogre changed himself into a tiny mouse and began to run around the room. The cat immediately sprung on him and ate him up!

Just then, the king's coach drove by the fine castle. The king, wanting to see who lived there, ordered the coach to go in. The cat, hearing the coach coming over the drawbridge, came out to meet them and said to the king, 'Welcome to the castle of my Lord, the Marquis of Carabas!'

'What? My Lord Carabas!' cried the king. 'Does this fine castle belong to you too? Let us see inside, if you please.'

The marquis helped the princess down from the coach and they followed the king inside the castle. There was a magnificent feast prepared in the Great Hall for the ogre. The king was perfectly charmed with the fine qualities of the marquis, as was the princess, who had fallen completely in love with him.

The king could see that his daughter was in love with the marquis and he was so impressed on seeing the vast estates and fine castle that the marquis owned that he insisted that the marquis and the princess get married that very day.

They lived happily ever after, and the cat became a great lord. He never had to chase mice again, although he sometimes did for fun!

THE
LITTLE
MERMAID

Far out in the deep ocean, where the water is as blue as the sky and as clear as crystal, there lived the Sea King and his six daughters. He lived in a beautiful castle with walls made of coral, windows of amber and a roof of shells that opened and closed as the water flowed over them. Inside each shell was a glittering pearl. The castle was surrounded by a garden of lovely, colourful sea plants and flowers and was filled with fish both large and small.

The Sea King's wife had died many years ago, so his aging mother kept house for him. She was very old and wise and looked after the sea princesses. The Sea King's youngest daughter was the most beautiful of all, with skin as delicate as a rose petal and eyes as blue as the sea. Like all sea people, she had no legs and her body ended in a fish's tail.

All day the princesses played in the halls of the castle or swam in the gardens. Each of the princesses had their own little garden in the castle grounds where they could dig and plant whatever they wished. One had a flower bed in the shape of a whale, another made her's like a shell, but the youngest princess's garden was shaped like the sun, which could be seen in calm weather, shining down like a great flower. Her garden was full of red and yellow flowers, like the rays of the sun at dusk.

The only thing the youngest princess cared for more than her pretty flowers was a beautiful marble statue of a handsome boy. It was carved out of pure white stone and had fallen to the bottom of the sea from a wrecked ship. She loved to hear stories of the world above the sea. Her grandmother would tell her about ships, towns, people and animals.

'When you have turned fifteen,' said her grandmother, 'you will be allowed to swim to the surface, to sit on the rocks and see the great ships, the forests and the towns.'

When the oldest sister turned fifteen, she swam to the surface to see the world above. When she returned, she told her younger sisters such wonderful tales. She told them of the moonlight on a sandbank, the twinkling lights of a town, the sound of music and voices and the ringing of the church bells. The youngest sister longed to see these wonderful things.

As the years passed, each sister turned fifteen, and was allowed to swim to the surface to see the world above. The second sister returned with tales of the sunset, the sky golden with red clouds scurrying across it and a flock of wild swans flying towards the sun.

The third sister was the bravest and swam up a wide river. She saw green hills, palaces and castles, forests and birds. She came across little children playing in the river and wanted to join them, but a little black animal came and barked at her so she swam away. It was a dog but she had never seen one before.

The fourth sister stayed in the ocean, but saw great ships as large as castles, their sails white in the sun. She swam with leaping dolphins and saw huge whales spurting water into the air.

The fifth sister's birthday was in the winter. When she swam to the surface, she saw enormous icebergs, like huge, glittering pearls. She sat on an iceberg and watched a storm, with dark clouds, rolling thunder and blue lightning, darting across the sky.

Once they had turned fifteen, the older sisters could swim to the surface whenever they wished. But after a few months, they decided they preferred to stay at home. However, in the evenings, the five older sisters would swim together to the surface and sing to the sailors on the ships about the delights of the ocean, but the sailors never understood, thinking it was just the wind.

Finally, the youngest sister turned fifteen. She bade farewell to her grandmother and swam to the surface. The sun was just setting as she raised her head above the waves and the sky was crimson and gold. A large ship with three masts sat in the water. It was stuck where it sat, for there was no breeze at all, and the sailors were making merry on the deck. Music was playing and the ship was lit up with lanterns.

The mermaid swam closer to the ship and looked in the cabin windows. She saw a number of finely dressed people inside. Among them was a handsome young prince. It was his sixteenth birthday and everyone on the ship was celebrating.

The young prince went up to the deck, and suddenly hundreds of rockets rose into the air. The little mermaid was amazed as she watched the fireworks exploding and falling like stars. How handsome the prince looked as he watched the fireworks!

As time passed, the sailors put out the lanterns, but still the little mermaid watched. The sea started to become restless and the waves grew higher. As the wind rose, the sailors unfurled the sails and the ship continued on its way, but still the mermaid followed. Soon dark clouds were racing across the sky and a terrible storm approached. The waves rose higher and higher.

Soon, the main mast groaned and then snapped off. Some of the planks of the ship came loose. The little mermaid could see the sailors holding on with all their might, but she could not see the handsome prince.

Suddenly, a flash of lightning crashed across the sky and the little mermaid saw him struggling in the water. As the prince sank down, she swam to him. His eyes were closed and he was not moving. She helped him to the surface and kept his head above the water until morning.

As the sun rose and the storm passed, there was no sign of the ship. They were in sight of land and so the little mermaid took the prince in to shore. There were green hills in the distance and a large white building like a church or a convent. The little mermaid laid the unconscious prince in the sand.

Then a bell rang in the distance and some young girls came out of the white building. The little mermaid swam out to sea and hid behind some rocks. One young girl walked to the beach, where she found the prince lying in the sand. The prince came to and smiled at the girl, and then many people came to help him. But the prince had no smile for the little mermaid, as he did not know she had rescued him. The little mermaid was very unhappy as the prince was led away into the white building. She returned home to the Sea King's castle.

After this, the little mermaid was always quiet and sad. She often swam to the beach where she had left the prince, but she never saw him. Her only comfort was to sit in her garden, but she let the flowers grow wild and it became very dark and gloomy.

At last she asked her sisters and they showed her where the prince's palace was. The little mermaid spent many days and nights in the sea near the palace, watching him. She saw him sailing his boat or walking on the shore. As she watched, she also saw other people and heard fisherman talking. She grew more and more fond of humans. Finally, she went to her grandmother and asked, 'Do humans live forever?'

'No,' replied her grandmother. 'They must die, and they do not live as long as we do. But when we die, we become the foam on the surface of the ocean and have no immortal souls. Humans have a soul that lives forever, even after they die.'

'So I will die and never hear the music of the waves or see the red sun. Is there nothing I can do to gain an immortal soul?' asked the little mermaid.

'Only if a man were to love you so much that you meant everything to him and he promised to be true to you alone,' replied her grandmother. 'But this could never happen, for we cannot walk among them. Be happy and swim in the ocean.'

The little mermaid was not content. She decided to visit the Sea Witch. She travelled past foaming whirlpools and bubbling mud. The Sea Witch's house lay in the middle of a strange forest full of plants with slimy branches like worms. The witch's house was made of bones and was surrounded by fat water snakes.

'I know what you want,' the Sea Witch said when she saw the little mermaid. 'You are very silly. You will get what you wish, but it will bring you nothing but sadness. You want legs like a human so the prince will fall in love with you and give you an immortal soul.'

The little mermaid nodded. The Sea Witch laughed and said, 'I will make you a potion. Swim to the shore before sunrise and drink it. Your tail will be replaced by legs, but every step will feel like you are standing on sharp knives. You can never be a mermaid again nor return to your home and family. And if the prince does not love you and marries another, you will become the foam on the waves. If you can bear that, I will help you.'

'I can bear it,' said the little mermaid.

'I must be paid,' said the Sea Witch. 'You have the sweetest voice of all the creatures of the sea. You must give it to me.'

The little mermaid was sad but she agreed. The witch prepared the potion and took the little mermaid's voice. The little mermaid returned home, where everyone was asleep. She took a flower from each of her sisters' gardens to remember them, and then swam away for the last time. She swam to shore and drank the potion, then swooned. The next thing she knew, the sun was up and the handsome prince was standing before her.

She realised that instead of her fish tail, she had legs. The prince asked where she was from but she could not answer, as she had no voice. The prince took her back to his castle. Every step felt as though she was walking on needles, but she walked gracefully. They dressed her in robes of silk and she was the most beautiful woman in the palace, but she could not speak.

The prince was charmed by her beauty and said she should stay with him always. She accompanied him everywhere he went. As the days passed, she loved the prince more and more, and he loved her as he would love a child, but he never thought to marry her.

'You are dear to me,' the prince told her, 'but there is only one woman in the world I could love. I was shipwrecked and the waves cast me to shore near a church. A young woman found me there and saved my life. She serves the church still.'

'He doesn't know it was me who saved him,' thought the little mermaid. 'I was the one who carried him to shore and I saw the pretty maid he loves more than me. But he shan't marry her as she serves the church.'

It was decided by the king and queen that the prince should marry. The daughter of a nearby king was to be his wife, so the little mermaid went on a ship with the prince and his court to visit them.

'I must visit her,' said the prince to the little mermaid, 'but they cannot force me to love her or marry her.'

One night as the ship was sailing, the little mermaid sat on the deck looking at the waves. She thought she could see her father's castle in the waters below. Then her sisters came to the surface and waved to her. She beckoned to them, but a cabin boy came by and so they dived down.

The next morning, the ship sailed into the beautiful harbour of the king. There was a big parade waiting to meet them. The princess had not yet arrived, as she was being educated in a church to learn the royal virtues.

At last she arrived and the little mermaid had to admit she was the most beautiful woman she'd ever seen. She was fair, with laughing blue eyes that shone with truth and purity.

When he saw her, the prince let out a cry and exclaimed, 'It was you who saved me when I lay shipwrecked on the beach! Oh, I am too happy! All my dreams have come true.'

He took the princess in his arms. The little mermaid felt as though her heart was breaking. She knew that when he married, she would change into the foam of the waves by the next morning and would never have an immortal soul.

That night, the prince was married, but the little mermaid only thought of the death that was coming to her. She was dressed in beautiful silks and she danced more gracefully than she had ever danced before. Even though it hurt her tender feet, she did not feel it, because the pain in her heart was much greater. The prince took his bride to his ship where the celebrations continued into the night. Then the ship grew quiet as everyone fell asleep.

The little mermaid leaned against the edge of the ship and looked towards the east, where the emerging sun would signal her end. She saw her sisters rising out of the water, but their beautiful long hair had been cut off.

'We have given our hair to the Sea Witch to help you so you won't die,' they told her. 'The witch gave us this knife. You must plunge it into the heart of the prince. When his blood hits your feet, you will become a mermaid again. Hurry; see the streaks of red in the sky? The sun will rise very soon!'

They gave the little mermaid the knife. She went to the prince's room and saw the prince and princess sleeping there. She kissed the prince's brow and looked at the sky, which was getting pinker and lighter all the time. She looked again at the prince and the knife trembled in her hand. Then she flung it into the sea, where it sank.

The little mermaid threw herself into the sea as the sun rose and thought she felt herself dissolving into foam. Then she realised she was being drawn up into the air, surrounded by hundreds of transparent beautiful creatures. The little mermaid saw that her body had become just like theirs. 'Where am I?' she asked, and realised she had a voice; a voice that was like a song.

'You are with the daughters of the air,' the creatures answered. 'A mermaid can only gain an immortal soul if she wins the love of a human being. But a daughter of the air can gain one through her good deeds. After we have striven to do good for three hundred years, we gain an immortal soul. You, poor mermaid, have tried with your whole heart to do good. You have suffered and endured and so you have joined the daughters of the air.'

The little mermaid looked up to the sun and felt her eyes filling with tears of joy. She saw the people on the ship looking for her. Unseen, she kissed the foreheads of the bride and the prince and then rose into the sky with the daughters of the air.

THE VALIANT TAILOR

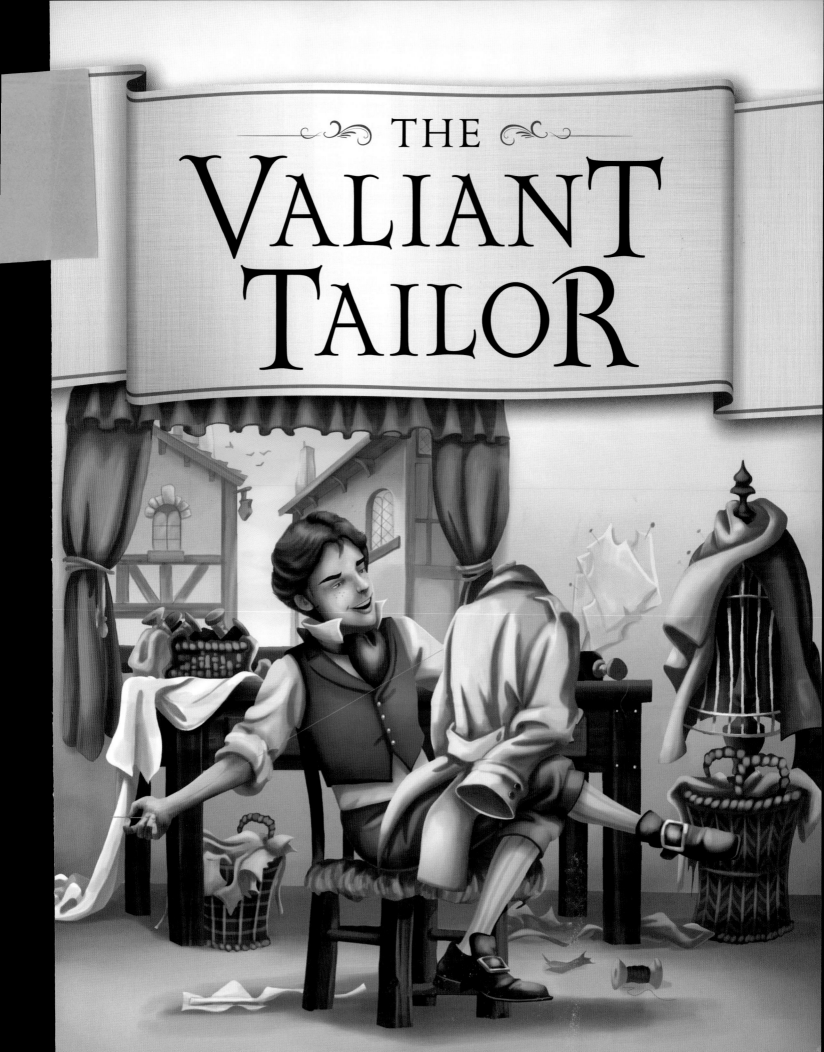

One summer's morning, a little tailor was sitting at his table near the window, working cheerfully away. As he worked, an old woman came down the street, shouting 'Good jams for sale! Good jams for sale, nice and cheap!'

This sounded like an excellent idea to the tailor, so he leaned out of the window and called out, 'Here, dear woman! I will buy some of your goods!'

The old woman climbed the step with a
heavy basket. The tailor made her un
which he inspected closely. He lifted
one. Finally, he said, 'This jam here s
me out four ounces please, dear won

The woman had hoped to make a good sale, so she grumbled
and complained as she weighed out the tiny amount, but the tailor
was very pleased. He cut some bread and spread the jam on it, then
laid it next to him while he continued working.

All the while, the smell of the sweet jam spread through the room. Soon some flies were attracted by the jam's lovely aroma and flew down to hover over the bread.

'Now then! Who invited you?' exclaimed the tailor, and he waved the uninvited flies away.

The flies, however, didn't seem to understand him, and returned in even larger numbers. Losing his patience, the tailor picked up a piece of leftover cloth from his table. He swatted away at the flies with the cloth, saying, 'Now you shall have it!'

When the tailor stopped swatting away, he counted the slain and found seven flies lying dead before him with their legs stretched out. 'This is indeed remarkable,' said the tailor, impressed at his own bravery. 'Why, the whole town should know of this!'

The tailor made himself a belt. He stitched on it, in large letters, 'Seven killed with one blow!' He put on his new belt and decided to go out into the world.

Before he went out, the tailor looked around the house to see what he could take with him. He found nothing but a hunk of soft cheese, which he put in his pocket. As he went out, he spied a bird caught in the thicket next to his door. He freed the bird and stowed it safely in his pocket with the cheese. Then he set out on his way.

The road the little tailor took led him up a mountain. When he reached the highest point, he saw a huge giant sitting there. The tailor walked up to him and said, 'Good day friend. I am on my way to try my luck in the world. Would you like to come with me?'

The giant looked at the tailor and screwed up his face. 'You little rascal! You miserable ragamuffin!' the giant said scornfully.

'Indeed?' said the little tailor, and he unbuttoned his coat and showed the giant his belt. The giant read, 'Seven killed with one blow!' and thought it meant men, not flies. He began to feel some respect for the tailor. But the giant still wanted to test the tailor, so he picked up a stone and squeezed it so hard that water come out of it.

'Can you do that?' asked the giant.

'Is that all?' asked the little tailor. 'A child could do that!' And he reached into his pocket and took out the cheese. He squeezed it until liquid ran out of it and asked, 'What do you think of that?'

The giant thought it was a stone in the tailor's hand and he didn't know what to say.

Then the giant picked up another stone and threw it so high that it nearly disappeared from sight. 'Can you do that?' asked the giant.

'That was a nice throw,' replied the little tailor, 'but the stone fell back to earth. I will throw one so high that it won't come down at all.' He felt in his pocket, took out the little bird and threw it into the air. The bird, happy that it was free, flew into the air and did not return.

'There is no doubt you can throw,' said the giant. 'But can you carry?' He took the tailor to a mighty oak tree that had fallen down and was lying on the ground. 'If you are strong enough, help me carry this tree out of the wood.'

'Gladly,' replied the tailor. 'You take the trunk on your shoulders and I will take the branches and leaves, as they are the most difficult to carry.'

The giant picked up the trunk on his shoulders, but the little tailor sat himself down in the branches. The giant, who could not look back with the trunk on his shoulders, carried the whole tree by himself. The tailor whistled as they went along.

Eventually, the giant cried out, 'I cannot carry it any further!' and dropped the tree. The tailor jumped off quickly and took hold of the branches as though he had been carrying it the whole time. 'You are such a big fellow, but you can't even carry a tree!' the tailor exclaimed.

They went on a little further and came to a cherry tree. The giant took hold of the top of the tree and pulled it down towards him so the tailor could pick some of the fruit. But when the tailor took hold of the tree, the giant let go, and the tailor was tossed up into the air. When he dropped down again, the giant said, 'How is this? Don't you have enough strength to hold on to a little tree like this?'

'That was no lack of strength,' replied the tailor. 'I jumped over the tree because I heard some huntsmen shooting over in that thicket. See if you can jump it, if you dare.'

The giant tried to jump over the tree but he got stuck in the branches. After he got himself down, the giant said to the tailor, 'If you are such a brave fellow, come to my cave and spend the night with my fellow giants.'

The tailor agreed and followed the giant to the cave. There were other giants there, sitting around a fire and roasting a sheep. The giant showed him where to sleep. However, the bed was very big, so the tailor did not stay in it but crept into a corner to sleep. Around midnight he awoke and saw the giant take up an iron bar and beat the bed with it. The giant thought he had put an end to the tailor.

As the sun rose the next morning, the giants went into the forest. The little tailor had arisen earlier and gone for a walk in the woods, and when the giants saw him walking towards them unhurt and cheerful, they were terribly frightened and ran away in a great hurry.

The little tailor walked on, following his nose. He walked for a long time until he came to a royal palace. As he was very weary, the little tailor lay on the grass in the palace courtyard and fell asleep. As he slept, the people of the palace came by and looked at him curiously. They read 'Seven killed with one blow!' on his belt, and thought he must be a great warrior. Some of the noblemen went and told the king about the little tailor and said that if a war should ever break out, he would be a useful and worthy man who should be pressed to stay at any price.

This idea pleased the king and he sent one of his men to ask the tailor if he would serve in the king's army. The messenger waited by the tailor's side until he awoke and then made him the offer. 'Why, this is why I have come here!' exclaimed the tailor. 'I am ready to enter the king's service.'

The little tailor was honourably received into the army and a special house was set apart for him. However, the rest of the soldiers were not pleased with this and wished the tailor a thousand miles away. 'What can we do?' the asked each other. 'If we quarrel and he should strike us, then seven of us will fall at each blow.'

The soldiers went as a group to the king and begged him to dismiss them all. 'We did not expect to serve with a man who could kill seven with one blow,' they said.

The king did not want to lose all his faithful soldiers and began to wish that he had never set eyes on the tailor. But he didn't dare dismiss a man who could kill the king and all his people, and then place himself on the throne.

The king thought for a long time, then sent for the tailor. He told the tailor that as he was so great a warrior, he had a proposal for him.

'There are two giants in a wood in my kingdom,' the king said. 'They cause great trouble with their robbery, murder, ravaging and burning and no one can go near them without putting themselves in danger. If you can kill these two giants, you shall have my only daughter for your wife and half the kingdom as your reward. I shall send one hundred horsemen with you to assist.'

'That would be something for a man like me!' thought the tailor. 'I shall subdue these giants,' he told the king, 'but I will not need the help of one hundred horsemen. He who can kill seven at one blow need not fear two.'

The tailor set out with the hundred horsemen. When he got to the edge of the wood, he told them to wait for him. He went into the wood and soon caught sight of the two giants asleep under a tree, snoring so hard that the branches shook.

The little tailor filled his pockets with stones and climbed the tree so that he was above the sleeping giants. Then he dropped one stone after the other on one giant's head. The giant awoke and pushed the other one. 'Why are you hitting me?' he asked angrily.

'It must be a dream,' said the other giant. 'I haven't touched you.'

Soon the two giants fell back to sleep. Again, the little tailor let more stones fall, this time on the head of the second giant. 'What is the meaning of this?' asked the second giant, waking up with a start. 'Why are you pelting me?'

'I have not thrown anything at you!' exclaimed the first giant, growling. The two giants argued for a while, but then grew quiet and fell back to sleep. The little tailor picked out the largest stone and threw it as hard as he could on to the head of the first giant.

'This is too much!' roared the first giant.

He jumped up and struck the second giant so hard that the whole tree shook. The second giant struck back with the same ferocity and the two giants got in such a rage that soon they were tearing up nearby trees and striking each other with all their might. At last, both giants fell down dead on the ground at the same time.

The little tailor jumped out of his tree, thinking it was lucky that neither of the giants tore up the tree he was in. He struck the giants a few times with his sword, then went back to the horsemen.

'The deed is done,' the tailor said. 'I have made an end to them both. It was a hard struggle and they uprooted many trees as they defended themselves, but I was the victor.'

The horsemen were amazed that the tailor was uninjured. Not believing his story, they rode into the forest to confirm it for themselves. They found the giants lying there, with uprooted trees all around them.

When he returned to the palace, the little tailor asked the king for his reward, but the king again tried to get rid of the hero. 'Before you can marry my daughter and take half my kingdom, you must perform another heroic act,' the king said. 'In another wood nearby there lives a unicorn that does great damage. You must catch him for me.'

'I fear one unicorn even less than I fear two giants!' replied the tailor. Taking some rope and an axe, he went alone into the wood. He soon saw the unicorn, who rushed towards the tailor as if it was going to run him through with its horn.

'Slowly, slowly. It can't be done quickly,' the tailor said to himself as the unicorn came charging towards him. He stood still until the unicorn was very close, then he nimbly sprung aside.

Now the clever tailor had been standing in front of a tree. The unicorn was running so fast that it could not stop in time and its horn became stuck in the trunk of the tree.

'Now I have caught you!' exclaimed the tailor. He placed the rope around the unicorn's neck and cut the trunk of the tree to free its horn. Then he led the beast away back to the king.

The king still did not want to give the tailor his reward. He stated that before the wedding could take place, the tailor must take the king's huntsmen to the forest and catch a wild boar that had been causing havoc. 'With pleasure!' said the tailor. 'Why, that's child's play.'

When the tailor and the huntsmen arrived at the forest, he instructed them to stay behind while he went on ahead. The huntsmen were very pleased at this, as they had tried to catch the boar before and had suffered for their trouble.

When the boar saw the tailor, it charged at him, its mouth foaming and its tusks gleaming. The nimble tailor rushed to a nearby chapel. He ran in the door, and then jumped out of a window on the other side of the building. The boar ran in after him, but the quick tailor shut the door on it, trapping it inside, as it was too big to jump through the window.

The tailor called the huntsmen, who took charge of the prisoner, and he returned to the king. The king was reluctantly obliged to fulfil his part of the bargain and he bequeathed the tailor his daughter's hand in marriage and half the kingdom. But if he had known of the tailor's low origins, he would have been even more upset.

One night after the wedding, the king's
daughter heard the tailor talking in his sleep. 'Now boy,
make me that waistcoat and patch those breeches or I'll rap my ruler
over your shoulders!' he muttered as he lay dreaming.

The king's daughter realised what low origins the tailor had and
told her father, begging him to get rid of her husband, who was just
a tailor. The king told her to leave her bedroom door open and when
the tailor was asleep, the king's men would carry him off and send
him on a ship to the other side of the world. However, the king's
armour-bearer was friendly with the tailor and told him of the plot.

The tailor went to bed that night. When his wife thought he was asleep, she opened the door. The tailor then began to murmur, 'Now boy, make me that waistcoat and patch those breeches or I'll rap my ruler over your shoulders! I've slain seven at one blow, killed two giants, caught a unicorn and trapped a wild boar, so why would a nobleman like me fear those who are standing outside my door?'

When they heard this, the guards outside the door ran away in terror and none of them would dare attack him again.

The king's daughter again thought her husband was a nobleman. Eventually, she grew to love him dearly and the little tailor one day became the king of the whole kingdom.

ALADDIN

Once there lived a young man named Aladdin. His father, a tailor, had died of grief because his son was so lazy and idle. Despite this, Aladdin did not mend his ways.

One day, Aladdin was approached by a stranger, who asked him his age and if he was the son of Mustafa, the tailor. 'I am, sir,' said Aladdin, 'but my father died some years ago.'

'I thought you looked like him!' exclaimed the stranger, who was a magician. 'I am your father's brother! Tell your mother I will come and visit.'

Aladdin ran home and told his mother about his new-found uncle. 'Your father had a brother,' she said, 'but we thought he died.'

However, she prepared a meal and welcomed the magician when he arrived. 'Don't be surprised that you don't know me,' said the magician. 'I have been out of the country for forty years.'

When his uncle heard that Aladdin had no profession, he offered to stock a shop for him to make his mother proud.

The following day, the magician took Aladdin out of the city. They journeyed for a long while until they reached the mountains. At last, they came to a narrow valley. 'We will go no further,' said the magician. 'Gather some sticks and I shall make a fire.'

When it was lit, the magician threw a powder on the fire and said some magic words. The ground shook and a stone slab with a brass ring was revealed. Aladdin tried to run away in fear but the magician stopped him. 'Don't be afraid,' said the magician. 'Beneath this stone lies a treasure. It shall be yours if you do exactly as I say.'

When he heard this, Aladdin forgot his fears. Following the instructions of the magician, he grasped the brass ring and pulled, saying the names of his father and grandfather. The stone came up easily and revealed a set of steps leading down.

'Go down,' said the magician to Aladdin. 'You will find a corridor leading to three large halls. Tuck in your gown and go through them. Do not touch the walls or you will instantly die. The halls lead to a garden of fruit trees. Go through the garden until you reach a stone terrace where a lighted lamp stands. Pour out the oil in the lamp and bring it back to me.'

The magician took off a ring and gave it to Aladdin. Aladdin followed his uncle's instructions. He picked up the lamp and walked back through the garden, taking some fruit off the trees as he went. Aladdin got back to the mouth of the cave and the magician cried out, 'Be quick and give me the lamp!'

But Aladdin refused, as he wasn't safely out of the cave yet. The magician flew into a terrible rage. He threw more powder on the fire and said some magic words. The stone rolled back into place, trapping Aladdin in the cave.

The magician fled far away to another country. He was not Aladdin's uncle, but an evil magician who had read of the lamp in his books. He knew it must be retrieved by the hand of another. The magician had picked Aladdin for this very reason and planned to kill him after he got the lamp.

For two days, Aladdin remained in the dark, crying. Realising he was stuck, he clasped his hands in prayer. As he did so, Aladdin rubbed the ring, which the magician had forgotten to take from him. Suddenly, an enormous genie rose up, saying, 'I am the slave of the ring! What is your wish?'

'Save me from here!' answered Aladdin. The stone rolled back and Aladdin climbed out and struggled home.

Aladdin told his mother about the magician's trickery. He showed her the lamp and the fruits, which were actually precious stones. His mother went to cook, but she had no food or money, so Aladdin said he would sell the lamp. It was very dirty, so he rubbed it with his sleeve to clean it. Instantly, a huge genie appeared. It bowed and asked, 'What will you have?'

'Fetch us something to eat!' said Aladdin. The genie conjured up a feast on silver bowls and cups. Aladdin told his mother about the cave, the ring and the lamp. At first she begged him to sell them, but Aladdin convinced her they should use them.

After they had eaten, they sold the silverware. Aladdin and his mother were able to live like this for several years. They ate the food provided by the genie, sold the silverware and lived off the money until they needed more.

One day, the sultan ordered everyone to stay inside and close their shutters. The princess was going to the bathhouse and no one was permitted to see her face. However, Aladdin hid near the bathhouse. He caught a glimpse of the princess's face when she lifted her veil as she walked in the door. She was so beautiful that Aladdin instantly fell in love with her.

Aladdin told his mother that he meant to ask the sultan for his daughter's hand in marriage. His mother laughed but Aladdin persuaded her to go to the sultan and present his request. She took the jewels from the trees in the cave with her, wrapped in a cloth.

For six days, Aladdin's mother went to sultan's hall, waiting for an audience. Finally, the sultan said to his vizier, 'I've seen that woman in the audience chamber for six days now, carrying something in that cloth. If she's here tomorrow, see what she wants.'

The next day, Aladdin's mother was summoned to the sultan. 'Tell me what you want, good woman,' said the sultan.

Aladdin's mother hesitated, so the sultan sent everyone away except for the vizier, promising he wouldn't take offence at what she was going to say. She told him of her son's love for his daughter and unfolded the jewels and presented them to the sultan.

The sultan was amazed by the priceless jewels. He turned to the vizier and said, 'See how much this man values my daughter? Surely I should allow them to marry.'

However, the vizier wanted his son to marry the princess. He convinced the sultan to wait three months before he gave his permission. The vizier hoped that he could make a richer gift and win the princess for his son. So the sultan agreed to Aladdin's proposal but told his mother that they must wait three months.

Aladdin waited. Two months went by, and then one day he discovered the townspeople rejoicing. 'Tonight the vizier's son is to marry the sultan's daughter!' they told him.

Aladdin fetched the lamp. He rubbed it and the genie appeared before him, saying, 'What is your will?'

'The sultan has broken his promise,' replied Aladdin. 'The princess marries the vizier's son. Bring them here tonight.'

'I obey, master,' said the genie.

Under the laws of the city, a couple were not married until they spent a night together. That night, the genie transported the princess and the vizier's son to Aladdin's house. 'Take this man and put him outside.' Aladdin said to the genie, 'Bring him in at daybreak.'

The genie took the vizier's son out, leaving the princess with Aladdin. 'Do not fear,' he said to her. 'You are promised as my wife and no harm shall come to you.'

The princess had a miserable night, as she was too frightened to sleep. In the morning, the genie fetched in the cold, shivering bridegroom and transported them back to the palace.

When the sultan came to wish them good morning, the vizier's son hid and the princess looked miserable. She wouldn't speak to her father but told her mother how she had been carried to a strange house where the vizier's son had been sent away. Her mother told her that it must have been a dream.

But the same thing happened the following night. The next morning, the princess told the sultan what had happened. The vizier's son refused to marry the princess, saying he'd rather die than go through another night like that.

Aladdin sent his mother to remind the sultan of his promise, but the sultan was reluctant to grant his permission. He told Aladdin's mother, 'Your son may marry my daughter, but he must send me forty basins of gold filled with jewels, carried by forty slaves, who are lead by another forty slaves, all splendidly dressed.'

Aladdin's mother went home, thinking all was lost. But Aladdin summoned the genie of the lamp and soon eighty slaves arrived, forty of them carrying gold basins filled with jewels. They set out for the palace with Aladdin's mother. Everyone crowded to see them.

Aladdin's mother entered the palace and bowed to the sultan. The sultan said, 'Tell your son I wait for him with open arms.'

Aladdin called the genie. 'I want a scented bath, an embroidered robe, a fine horse and twenty slaves. I need six slaves to wait on my mother and ten thousand gold pieces in ten purses.' And it was done.

Aladdin mounted his horse and rode to the palace, followed by slaves throwing gold pieces to the cheering crowd. The sultan welcomed Aladdin and asked him to marry his daughter that day, but Aladdin said he had to build a palace for the princess first.

Aladdin said to the genie, 'Build a palace of finest marble set with precious stones. Put a large domed hall in the middle with walls of gold and silver. Put windows of diamonds and rubies in each wall. There must be stables, horses, grooms and slaves.'

The palace was finished the next day. Aladdin and his mother went to the sultan's palace. They were met by musicians and dancers. The princess was charmed by the handsome Aladdin. The princess told him that she was very happy to obey her father and marry him. They danced at the wedding feast until midnight and then returned to Aladdin's palace.

The next day, Aladdin invited the sultan to see the palace. The sultan was astounded, but the jealous vizier hinted that it must be the work of magic. However, Aladdin had won the heart of the sultan, who made Aladdin the captain of his armies. Over the next few years, Aladdin lived happily with the princess and won several battles for the sultan, but he remained courteous and modest.

However, far away, the evil magician remembered Aladdin. He was furious when he heard that Aladdin had escaped, married a princess and was living in great honour and wealth instead of perishing. This could have only happened with the lamp and so the magician set out to seize it for himself. He was determined to see Aladdin ruined.

When he arrived in the town, the magician discovered that Aladdin had gone hunting. The magician went to the market and bought a dozen new lamps. He put them in a basket and dressed as a peddler. He made his way towards Aladdin's palace, crying out, 'New lamps for old!' The townspeople laughed at this poor trade.

The princess was sitting in the garden when she heard the crowd laughing. She sent a slave to find out what the fuss was about. When she heard that a peddler was exchanging old lamps for brand new ones, she told the slave to take the old lamp from the shelf and exchange it. Now this was the magic lamp, which Aladdin could not take hunting with him.

Amidst the jeers of the crowd, the slave made the exchange. The magician ran out of the city gates. He waited until night and then rubbed the lamp. At his command, the genie carried the palace, the princess and the magician far away.

The sultan was shocked that Aladdin's palace was gone. He asked the vizier what had happened and the jealous vizier said that it was magic, for which the penalty was death. The sultan sent soldiers out for Aladdin, who bound him in chains. But the people loved Aladdin and they followed them to the palace.

The sultan ordered the executioner to cut off Aladdin's head, but the crowd forced their way in to rescue him. They were so threatening that the sultan ordered the executioner to stop. Aladdin begged to know what he had done. 'Where is my daughter?' demanded the sultan. 'Find her or you will lose your head!'

Aladdin begged the sultan to give him forty days to find her. If he couldn't, he promised to return and the sultan could do what he wished. The sultan agreed and Aladdin went to find the princess.

Aladdin wandered for several days. No one could tell him what happened to his palace. He came to a river and in despair decided to throw himself in. He knelt to pray, but as he did, he rubbed the magic ring, which he still wore. The genie of the ring appeared and asked him what his wish was. 'Bring my palace back!' said Aladdin.

'I do not have that power,' answered the genie of the ring. 'Only the genie of the lamp can do that.'

'Can you take me to my palace outside my wife's window?' asked Aladdin.

Aladdin found himself far away under the princess's window. When she saw Aladdin again, the princess was delighted and kissed him joyfully. 'Tell me, my love,' asked Aladdin, 'what happened to the old lamp that I left on the shelf?'

'It is all my fault!' exclaimed the princess. She told how she had exchanged the lamp. 'The magician has it,' she said. 'He wishes to marry me and says that my father beheaded you, but I refuse him.'

Aladdin went into a nearby town, bought a powder and snuck into the palace. 'Put on a beautiful dress and pretend you have forgotten me,' he told the princess. 'Invite him to eat with you and ask to try some wine. I will tell you what to do.'

The princess dressed in her finest clothes and received the magician. 'I have decided to mourn for Aladdin no more,' she said. 'Eat with me and let us try some of the wines of your country.'

The magician was dazzled by her beauty and smiles and ran to the wine cellar. Meanwhile, the princess put some of Aladdin's powder into the magician's cup. The magician returned, drank the wine from his cup and fell down dead. Aladdin quickly retrieved the lamp and asked the genie to set things right. How pleased the sultan was to see the palace returned and his daughter safe!

Aladdin thought he could live in peace, but it wasn't to be. The magician's brother was even more wicked and cunning and came to avenge him. He stole a holy woman's clothes and went to Aladdin's palace, his face hidden by a veil. A crowd gathered around him as he went, thinking he was a holy woman, and asked for a blessing.

The princess heard the crowd and told a servant to see what was going on. The servant said it was a holy woman who could cure people with her touch. The princess invited the false holy woman to the palace. The magician's brother looked around the palace and said it was very fine. 'However,' he said, 'it is lacking something.'

'What is that?' asked the princess.

'Hang an egg of the mystical bird, the roc, from the dome and it would be the wonder of the world,' answered the false holy woman.

After this, the princess thought of nothing but a roc's egg. She told Aladdin that her joy in the palace was ruined because it didn't have a roc's egg. 'If that is all, you shall soon be happy,' he replied.

Aladdin rubbed the lamp and commanded the genie to bring him a roc's egg. But the genie gave a shriek that shook the palace.

'Haven't I done enough for you?' demanded the genie. 'Now you want the egg of the fearsome roc! This request doesn't come from you, but from the evil magician's brother! He is here, disguised as a holy woman! He has requested this, hoping you would be killed by the roc. This man intends to murder you.'

Aladdin told the princess that his head ached and he wished the holy woman to cure him. But when the false holy woman came near, Aladdin seized his dagger and slew him. The princess was horrified, but Aladdin said, 'This is no holy woman! This is the magician's evil brother!' and he told her how she had been tricked.

After this, Aladdin and the princess lived a long and happy life. When the sultan died, Aladdin succeeded him as ruler and reigned with the princess for many happy years.

TOM THUMB

There once lived a poor woodsman and his wife. Every evening, the woodsman would sit next to the fire while his wife would spin at her spinning wheel.

One evening, the woodsman said to his wife, 'How lonely it is for just you and me to sit here by ourselves without any children to play about and amuse us. Other people's houses seem so happy and merry with their children and ours is so quiet.'

'How very true,' sighed his wife. 'How happy I should be if I had even one child! Even if it were as little as my thumb, I would still be very happy and love it dearly.'

Now it came to pass that the good woman's wish was fulfilled, for not long after, she had a little boy. He was healthy and strong and perfect in every way, except he was no bigger than a thumb.

'He is just what we wished for,' said his parents, 'and we will love him very much.'

His parents named him Tom Thumb. They gave him plenty of food, yet despite all their efforts, he stayed the same size as he was when he was born. Still, his eyes were sharp and sparkling and he was clever and quick, so he succeeded in all that he did.

One day, his father was preparing to go into the forest to cut some wood. He was in a hurry and muttered, 'Oh, if only I had someone to bring the cart to meet me, for I need to hurry.'

'Oh Father,' cried Tom, 'I can bring the cart to you. It shall be in the woods by the time you need it.'

His father laughed kindly and said, 'Now Tom, how can you do that? You cannot reach the horse's reins.'

'Don't worry,' replied Tom. 'If Mother will only harness the horse to the cart, I will sit in the horse's ear and tell him which way to go.'

'Well,' replied his father, 'we will try it this once and see how it goes.'

When the time came, his mother harnessed the horse and set Tom in its ear. Little Tom cried out, 'Gee-up!' and 'Whoa!' and the horse went along just as well as if the woodsman himself was driving it.

Now it happened that as they were turning a corner and Tom was calling out, 'Gee-up!', two strangers came along. 'What an odd thing that is!' exclaimed one. 'There is a cart and the driver is calling to the horse, but he is nowhere to be seen!'

'That is very strange,' agreed the other stranger. 'Let's follow the cart and see where it goes.'

So the two men went on into the wood, following the cart. At last, the cart came to where the woodsman was cutting trees in the forest. When Tom saw his father, he called out, 'See Father, I am here with the cart all safe and sound! Now take me down.'

His father took hold of the horse's bridle with one hand and lifted Tom out of the horse's ear with the other hand and put him down on a tree stump, where Tom sat, happy as can be.

The two strangers were watching. They were struck dumb with wonder when they saw little Tom Thumb. Finally, one turned to the other and said, 'That little chap could make us a fortune if we were to show him in town for money! We must buy him.'

So they went up to the woodsman and asked, 'How much would you sell the little man for? He would be far better off with us than with you and we shall make sure he comes to no harm.'

'No indeed,' replied the woodsman. 'He is my own flesh and blood and he is dearer to me than all the silver and gold in the world.'

But Tom had heard what the men said. Climbing up his father's coat and perching himself on his shoulder, Tom whispered, 'Take the money, Father. It will do you and Mother a great deal of good and I shall return to you soon.'

After a great deal of persuasion from the two men, the woodsman agreed to let Tom go with them.

'Where would you like to sit?' asked one of the men.

'Oh, put me on the brim of your hat,' replied Tom. 'I can walk about and view the country and I'll be in no danger of falling off.'

So they did as he asked and paid the woodsman his gold. When Tom had said farewell to his father, they set off.

They walked and walked until the sun started to set. Then Tom said, 'Let me down, as I am tired.'

The strangers were not happy about letting Tom down and it was with some difficulty that he finally persuaded them. Finally, the man took off his hat and set Tom down in a ploughed field next to the road.

Tom immediately ran off into the field along a furrow. He ran and ran, and just as he was about to be seized by one of the men, he slipped into an old mouse hole.

'Good night sirs!' Tom cried out loudly. 'I'm off! You can go home without me!'

The men cursed and raged at Tom. They found a sharp stick and poked it into the hole, but it was in vain. Tom just crawled further until the stick could not reach him. At last it grew dark. The men were forced to go on their way without their prize, angry as can be.

When Tom was sure they had left, he crept out of the hole. He tried to cross the ploughed field but the furrows were so high that he was in danger of falling down in the dark and breaking his neck. At last, he came across a large empty snail shell.

'How lucky,' Tom thought. 'I can sleep here safely through the night and then make my way when the sun comes up.'

Tom crept inside the shell and settled himself down. But as he was falling asleep, he heard some more men pass by the field. There were two of them and they were talking to each other.

'How shall we rob the rich old parson of his gold and silver?' one said to the other.

'I can tell you how!' Tom cried out at the top of his voice.

'What was that?' said one of the thieves, startled. 'I'm sure I heard someone speak!'

The two thieves stood listening and Tom spoke again. 'Take me with you,' he said, 'and I shall show you how to get the good parson's money!'

'Where are you?' asked the confused thieves, looking around.

Tom crawled out of the snail shell and replied, 'Look down to the ground and you will see where I am.'

The two thieves found him and picked him up. 'You little elf!' they exclaimed. 'What could you do for us?'

'Why, I can easily sneak between the iron bars over the windows of the parson's house,' replied Tom. 'I can pass you whatever you would like.'

'That's a good idea,' said the thieves. 'Come along and let's see what you can do.'

When they came to the parson's house, Tom slipped through the window bars into the main room. Then he cried out at the top of his voice, 'Will you take all that is here?'

The two thieves were frightened and whispered back to him, 'Speak more softly! Be quiet, so you don't wake anybody!'

But Tom acted as though he didn't understand them. Again, he cried out loudly, 'What would you like me to take? Shall I throw it out the window to you?'

Tom shouted so loudly that the maid, who was sleeping in the next room, woke up. She raised herself up on her elbow, listening.

The two thieves had run off a short distance in fear, but at last they plucked up their courage and crept back, thinking that Tom must be playing a joke on them.

They whispered softly to Tom, 'Now let us have no more of your pranks and pass out some of the money.'

Then Tom called out as loud as he could, 'Very well! Hold out your hands and I will give it all to you!'

At this, the maid sprang out of bed and ran to open the door. The two thieves ran off as though a wolf were at their tails. The maid looked into the room but couldn't see anything in the dark, so she went off to get a lamp.

By the time the maid returned, Tom had slipped out the window into the barn. She looked everywhere, searching every hole and corner. Finding nobody, she went back to bed, thinking it was a dream.

Tom crawled into the hay loft and found a snug place to sleep. He lay down, meaning to sleep until daylight and then find his way home to his parents. But what other troubles would befall him!

The maid got out of bed at dawn to feed the cows. Going straight to the hay loft, she picked up a bundle of hay. It happened to be the very heap on which Tom Thumb lay fast asleep. He slept on until he awoke with a start and found himself in the mouth of a cow, which had eaten him along with the hay!

Tom soon realised where he was and had to have all his wits about him to avoid the cow's teeth. At last he was swallowed by the cow and ended up in her stomach. 'It is very dark!' he exclaimed. 'They forgot to build windows in here!'

Tom tried to make the best of his bad luck but he did not like his new quarters at all. More and more hay kept coming in and the space left for him grew smaller and smaller. At last, he cried out as loudly as he could, 'No more hay! No more hay for me!'

The maid happened to be milking the cow. She heard someone speak but saw no one. Sure it was the same voice she'd heard the night before, the maid was so frightened that she fell off her milking stool. She picked herself up out of the dirt and ran to get the parson.

'Sir, sir! The cow is talking!' she exclaimed.

'Surely you are mad!' said the parson. But he went with her to see what the matter was.

They had barely entered the barn when Tom called out, 'Don't bring me any more hay!'

Then the parson was also frightened. Thinking the cow was bewitched, he ordered his man to kill it. The cow's stomach was thrown on to the dung heap with Tom still lying inside.

Tom set about trying to climb out of the stomach through the hay, which was not an easy task. At last, just as he was about to get his head out, more bad luck befell him. A hungry wolf jumped out and swallowed the stomach in one gulp, with Tom still inside. The wolf ran into the woods.

Despite this, Tom was not disheartened. Thinking the wolf would not mind having a chat as he went along, Tom called out, 'My friend, I can show you where you can get a splendid meal!'

'Where is it to be had?' asked the surprised wolf.

'I can show you a house,' said Tom, and he described his own home. 'Crawl through the drain into the kitchen. There you will find the pantry full of cakes, ham, beef, bacon, chicken and everything that you could wish for.'

The wolf did not need to be told twice. That night, he went to Tom's house and squeezed in through the drain into the kitchen. There he feasted to his heart's content. When the wolf had eaten all that he could, he tried to squeeze his way out through the drain. But he had eaten so much that he could not fit through to get out.

This was what Tom had reckoned on. Now he began to make a great noise, singing as loudly as he could.

'Would you be quiet?' said the wolf. 'You will wake everybody in the house up!'

'Look here!' cried Tom. 'You've had your fun and now it's my turn!' Again he began to sing at the top of his voice.

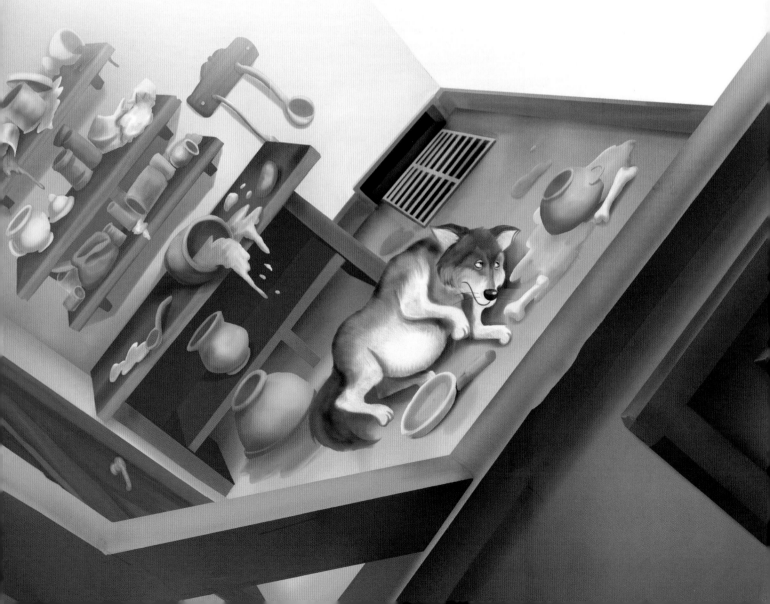

The woodsman and his wife were woken by the noise. Peering through a crack in the door, they saw the wolf in the kitchen. The woodsman ran for his axe and the wife picked up a scythe.

'Stay behind me!' said the woodsman to his wife. 'I shall give him a blow but you must cut at him if I miss.'

Hearing the woodsman's voice, Tom cried out, 'Father, Father! I am here! The wolf has swallowed me!'

'Heaven be praised!' cried the woodsman. 'We have found our son again!'

He told his wife not to use the scythe in case she should hurt Tom and then he aimed a blow at the wolf's head and dispatched him. They cut the wolf open and set Tom free.

'What fears we had for you!' said Tom's father.

'Yes Father, I have travelled a good deal of the world and I am most glad to breathe fresh air again!' replied Tom.

'Why, where have you been?' asked his mother.

'Oh, I have been inside a mouse hole and in a snail shell and down a cow's throat and in a wolf's belly!' said Tom. 'But here I am, safe and sound. Now I think I will stay at home.'

'And we will not part with you for all the gold in the world!' his parents cried, and they kissed and hugged their dear little son and gave him food, for he was hungry, and fetched him new clothes, for his old ones were all ruined.

And Tom stayed home with his father and mother in peace, for though he had been so great a traveller and loved to tell the story of his journey, he would always agree that there's no place like home!

SNOW WHITE
AND THE
SEVEN DWARFS

Once upon a time, in the middle of winter when the snowflakes were falling from the sky, a queen sat sewing at her window, which had a frame of black ebony wood. As she sewed, she looked out at the snow and accidentally pricked her finger with the needle. Three drops of blood fell from the open window into the snow.

As she looked at the brilliant red on the white snow, the queen thought to herself, 'If only I had a child with skin as white as snow, with lips as red as blood and hair as black as ebony.'

Soon after that, the queen had a little daughter. She was named Snow White, because her skin was as white as snow, her lips as red as blood and her hair as black as ebony. Alas, soon after the child was born, the queen died.

A year later, the king remarried. His new wife was a beautiful woman, but she was also proud and vain. She could not bear the thought that someone else might be more beautiful than her. She had a magic mirror which she looked into every morning, and asked:

'Mirror, mirror, on the wall,

Who in this land is the fairest of all?'

The mirror would always reply:

'You, Queen, are the fairest of all.'

The queen was always satisfied, because she knew that the mirror had to tell the truth.

As the years passed and Snow White grew up, she became more and more beautiful. Eventually, she was even more beautiful than the queen herself. One day, the queen asked her mirror:

'Mirror, mirror, on the wall,

Who in this land is the fairest of all?'

The mirror answered:

'You, my queen are fair, it's true,

But Snow White is a thousand times fairer than you.'

When the queen heard this, she turned white with fury and jealousy. From that time on, whenever the queen looked at Snow White, her heart heaved in her breast. So great was her hatred that she had no peace, day or night, and her envy and pride grew like a weed.

Finally, she summoned a huntsman and ordered, 'Take Snow White out into the woods. I never want to see her again. Kill her, and bring me her heart as proof she is dead!'

The huntsman took Snow White out into the woods. But when he drew his knife, Snow White begged him to spare her life. The huntsman took pity on her and could not bear to harm her. 'Run away, poor child,' he said to her.

'The wild animals will soon devour her,' the huntsman thought sadly, but he was relieved that he did not have to kill her. He spied a young boar in the forest and killed it, cut out its heart and took it back to the queen as proof of Snow White's death. The queen was very pleased.

Poor Snow White was all alone in the great forest. She looked around, and then she began to run. She ran over sharp stones and through thorn bushes and she saw wild animals, but she came to no harm.

Snow White ran for as long as she could, until it was almost evening. Then she saw a little cottage in the forest, so she went inside to rest. Everything in the cottage was very small but it was very neat and clean. There was a table set with seven places, all with little plates, mugs, spoons, knives and forks. A little loaf of bread sat on every plate and each little mug had some wine in it. Against the wall were seven little beds.

Snow White was so hungry and thirsty that she ate a piece of each loaf and drank some wine from each mug. After that, she tried all the beds, but some were too short and some were too hard, until she tried the seventh bed, which suited her very well. She lay down and fell asleep.

When it was dark outside, the owners of the cottage came home. They were seven dwarfs who dug and mined in the mountains for gold and silver. The dwarfs lit their seven candles and saw that someone had been in their house, for things had moved from where they left them.

The first cried, 'Who has been eating from my plate?'

The second cried, 'Who has been eating my bread?'

The third cried, 'Who has been sitting on my chair?'

The fourth cried, 'Who has been using my fork?'

The fifth cried, 'Who has been cutting with my knife?'

The sixth cried, 'Who has been meddling with my spoon?'

The seventh cried, 'Who has been drinking from my mug?'

Then the first dwarf looked around and exclaimed, 'Who has been lying on my bed?'

The other dwarfs all cried out that someone had been lying on their beds too. But the seventh dwarf saw Snow White asleep on his bed and called the others to come and see her. They looked at her by the light of their seven candles and exclaimed, 'Good heavens! What a lovely girl she is!' They didn't wake her up but let her sleep through the night.

The next morning, Snow White woke up and saw the seven dwarfs. She was frightened, but soon realised they were friendly and introduced herself. She told them how her stepmother tried to kill her but the huntsman had spared her life and she had run until she found their cottage.

The dwarfs said, 'If you will keep house for us, you can live here and we will take care of you.' Snow White agreed with all her heart.

Each day, the dwarfs went to work in the mountains, digging for gold and silver, while Snow White stayed home alone. The dwarfs warned her, 'The queen will soon discover where you are. Make sure you don't let anyone in.'

The queen believed Snow White was dead and that she was the most beautiful again. She went to her magic mirror and asked:

'Mirror, mirror, on the wall,

Who in this land is the fairest of all?'

The mirror answered:

'You, my queen are fair, it's true,

But Snow White, beyond the mountains, with the seven dwarfs,

Is still a thousand times fairer than you.'

This upset the queen, as she realised that Snow White was still alive. She couldn't bear the thought that someone was more beautiful than her, so she dressed herself up as an old peddler woman. In this disguise, she went to the house of the seven dwarfs and knocked at the door. She called out, 'Beautiful wares for sale!'

Snow White looked out the window and asked what was for sale. 'Fine laces in all colours!' replied the old peddler.

'She looks like an honest woman,' thought Snow White, and she opened the door. She bought a pretty bodice lace.

'Let me lace you up,' said the disguised queen, but she pulled so hard that Snow White could not breathe and she fell down as though she were dead.

'You used to be more beautiful,' laughed the queen, and went on her way.

Soon after, the seven dwarfs came home. When they saw poor Snow White lying there, they lifted her up and saw the tight lace. They quickly cut it and Snow White began to breathe again. When the dwarfs heard what happened, they said to Snow White, 'That old peddler woman was no other than the queen! Make sure you let no one in when you are alone.'

When she got home, the queen went to her magic mirror and asked:

'Mirror, mirror, on the wall,

Who in this land is the fairest of all?'

The mirror answered:

'You, my queen are fair, it's true,

But Snow White, beyond the mountains, with the seven dwarfs,

Is still a thousand times fairer than you.'

The queen was furious that Snow White was still alive. Using her witchcraft, she made a poisoned comb. She disguised herself as another old woman and went to the dwarfs' house. She knocked at the door and called out, 'Fine wares for sale!'

Snow White looked out the window and said, 'I am not to let anyone in.'

'Surely you can take a look,' replied the old woman, pulling out the poisoned comb. Snow White liked it so much that she agreed and opened the door. The old woman offered to comb her hair, but as soon as the comb touched her, Snow White fell down unconscious.

'Now you are finished!' cried the queen, and went on her way.

Soon the seven dwarfs came home and saw Snow White lying on the ground as though dead. They pulled the poison comb out of her hair and Snow White awoke and told them what happened. Again, they warned her not to open the door to anyone.

The queen went home and again asked her magic mirror:

'Mirror, mirror, on the wall,

Who in this land is the fairest of all?'

The mirror answered:

'You, my queen are fair, it's true,

But Snow White, beyond the mountains, with the seven dwarfs,

Is still a thousand times fairer than you.'

The queen flew into a rage. 'Snow White shall die!' she shouted.

She went to her secret room and made a poisoned apple. It had beautiful red cheeks and an alluring smell. Anyone would be tempted to eat it. Disguising herself as a peasant woman, the queen went to the house of the seven dwarfs and knocked at the door.

Snow White looked out the window. When she saw the peasant woman, she said, 'I am not to let anyone in.'

'I don't mind,' said the peasant woman. 'Don't worry, I will easily be able to sell my apples in time. In fact, let me give you this pretty one as a gift.'

'I cannot accept anything,' replied Snow White.

'What are you afraid of?' asked the peasant woman. 'Here, I'll cut it in two. You can eat one half and I shall have the other.'

The queen had cleverly made the apple so that only half was poisoned. She cut it in two and ate some of the unpoisoned half.

Snow White longed for the apple, and when she saw the peasant woman eating it, she could no longer resist. She took the apple and bit into it, but she barely had it in her mouth before she fell down dead.

'This time the dwarfs can't wake you!' the queen laughed.

The queen went home and asked the magic mirror:

'Mirror, mirror, on the wall,

Who in this land is the fairest of all?'

The mirror answered:

'You, Queen, are the fairest of all.'

And the queen was very pleased.

When the dwarfs came home, they found Snow White lying on the ground, not breathing. They tried to wake her, they washed her face and hands, they combed her hair, but nothing worked. She was dead. They mourned and cried for three days, but she still looked as fresh as a living person with her red cheeks.

'We cannot bury her in the dark ground,' the dwarfs said. They made a transparent coffin of glass so they could still see her. Then they put the coffin in a beautiful spot in the hills and one of the dwarfs always watched over her. Even the animals of the woods came to mourn for her.

Snow White lay in the coffin for a long, long time, but she just looked like she was asleep. She was still as white as snow, as red as blood and as black as ebony.

One day, a handsome prince entered the woods. He needed shelter for the night, and came to the dwarfs' cottage. He saw the coffin with Snow White in it. The prince immediately fell in love with Snow White, and begged the dwarfs to let him take the coffin. He offered them money, but the dwarfs said, 'We would not part with her for anything in the world.'

In despair, the prince said, 'Then please give the coffin to me. I cannot live without seeing her.'

Seeing his distress, the dwarfs took pity on him and gave him the coffin.

The moment the prince lifted the coffin to carry it home with him, the piece of poisoned apple was jolted out of Snow White's mouth and she awoke.

'Where am I?' Snow White asked.

The prince told her what had happened and said, 'I love you more than anything. Come with me to my father's castle and become my wife.'

Snow White saw the love in the prince's eyes and agreed. Their wedding was planned with great splendour.

Snow White's stepmother was invited to the prince's wedding.
After she put on her beautiful clothes, she asked the magic mirror:

'Mirror, mirror, on the wall,

Who in this land is the fairest of all?'

The mirror answered:

'You, my queen are fair, it's true,

But the young bride is a thousand times fairer than you.'

The queen was furious when she saw the bride was Snow White.
She died soon after, destroyed by her hatred and envy. Snow White
and the prince reigned happily for many years. They often visited
the dwarfs in the mountains, who had been so kind to Snow White
in her time of need.

THE
MUSICIANS
OF BREMEN

A farmer once owned an old donkey. The donkey had worked faithfully for his master for many years. He'd carried huge sacks of wheat up the hill to the mill and bags of flour back down again, pulled heavily laden carts great distances and been ridden into town and back by the farmer's wife and children.

As he grew older, the poor donkey's strength began to fail him and he was no longer able to perform all the tasks that the farmer set him. With each day that passed, the donkey became more and more unfit for the hard work for which the farmer needed him.

At last, the farmer decided that it was time for him to get rid of the poor old donkey, as he could not afford to keep the beast if he could not perform his duties. However, the old donkey overheard the farmer talking to his wife about whether he should turn the donkey out or put an end to him. The donkey, guessing that his future at the farm looked grim, decided he would run away.

After some thought, the donkey resolved that he would take the road to the town of Bremen, famous for its freedom, where he could make his own living as a town musician. So off he headed down the road to that great city.

After the donkey had walked for a little way, he came across a dog lying down next to the road. The dog was panting as though he was tired after running a long distance.

'Hello friend,' said the donkey. 'Why are you panting and so out of breath?'

'Alas!' replied the dog. 'Now that I'm old and getting weaker all the time, my master has decided that I can no longer make myself useful when he's hunting. He decided get rid of me, but I escaped and ran away. I've been travelling such a long way, but I have no idea how I am going to earn my livelihood.'

'I've got an idea,' said the donkey. 'My master was also going to get rid of me because I was getting too old to work for him. I have also run away and I am making my way to Bremen, where I will become a town musician. Why don't you join me and we shall earn our living by making music together?'

The dog happily agreed, and so the two animals continued down the road together, talking about their plans to become musicians.

After the donkey and the dog had gone a little further, they spied a cat sitting by the road, looking as miserable as a cat could possibly look.

'Hello dear lady,' said the donkey. 'Why do you look so very sad?'

'You'd look miserable too if you were in danger of being thrown in the well,' replied the cat. 'Now that I am getting old, my teeth and claws are becoming blunt. I'd much prefer to lie by the kitchen fire and purr and sleep instead of running about the house chasing mice all day. My mistress was going to get rid of me because I was of no further use to her, so I ran away. But now I don't know what is going to become of me.'

'Why don't you come with us to Bremen?' suggested the donkey. 'The dog and I have also run away from our masters because we are too old and so we are going to try earning our way by becoming town musicians. You are bound to be an excellent night-time singer!'

The cat was very pleased with this idea and so the three animals continued down the road together towards Bremen.

The donkey, dog and cat had walked a little further when they saw a rooster perched on a farm gate. He was loudly crowing with all his might, creating an enormous racket.

'Bravo!' cried the donkey. 'What a wonderful performance! But tell me, why are you making all this fuss?'

'I have been a good rooster and foretold fine weather for wash-day,' said the rooster, 'but instead of getting any thanks, I heard that my mistress has company coming for Sunday lunch. She has told the cook to cut off my head tomorrow and cook me in a soup for them to eat! So here I am, crowing with all my might while I still can.'

'Goodness me!' exclaimed the donkey. 'You had better come along with us, good sir. Anything would be better than staying to have your head removed! Who knows? If we can all sing in tune, your powerful voice will be a very pleasing addition to our performance.'

The rooster was very happy to accept this offer and so he joined them on their travels to Bremen. The four animals went on down the road together, quite jolly.

However, as they went along, the four friends realised that they could not reach Bremen in one day. As night approached, the travellers came to a wood. They talked together and decided that they would spend the night in the woods and then continue on to Bremen the next morning.

The donkey and the dog lay down to sleep on the ground under a great tree. The cat climbed up into the branches of the tree for her rest. The rooster flew up to the top of the tree, as that was the safest place for him to perch for the night.

As was his habit, the rooster looked around on all sides to make sure all was well before he settled down to sleep. As he was looking out into the wood, the rooster spied a little light off through the trees, bright and shining.

'I see a light!' the rooster called down to his friends. 'There must be a house nearby, as the light does not seem very far away!'

'If that is so,' said the donkey, 'it would be best if we got up and investigated. After all, this wood is not the best place to sleep, especially when there is somewhere close by that might be much better! They might have a nice warm stable and some fresh hay for me to munch on.'

'I wouldn't mind a bone or two either, or a bit of meat to eat,' said the dog.

'Maybe there's a cosy basket by the fire and a piece of fish to dine on,' said the cat.

'Or a snug hen house with some tasty corn for me to peck at,' said the rooster.

So the four friends decided they would seek out better quarters for the night. They set off together into the woods towards where the rooster had seen the light.

As they came closer, the light shone brighter and brighter until they could see a snug little house, all lit up. Now, it turned out that this was a house in which a gang of fearsome robbers lived.

The donkey, being the tallest, went up to the window and peeked in.

'Well, donkey, what do you see?' asked the dog.

'What do I see? I see a large table laid out with all kinds of splendid things to eat,' replied the donkey. 'I also see a gang of robbers sitting around the table, eating and drinking and looking very comfortable.'

'That sounds like it would be very suitable for us,' said the rooster.

'Yes indeed,' said the donkey. 'Now if only we could get in there.'

The four friends consulted together on the best way to get the robbers out of the house. After a great deal of discussion, they hit on a plan.

The donkey stood up on his hind legs with his front legs resting on the window sill for support. The dog climbed up on to the donkey's back and then the cat scrambled up on to the dog's shoulders. Finally, the rooster flew up and perched himself on top of the cat's head.

When they were all ready, the donkey gave a signal and the animals began to perform their music. The donkey brayed loudly, the dog barked furiously, the cat meowed at the top of her voice and the rooster crowed deafeningly.

Then, the four animals crashed in through the window, tumbling amongst the broken glass with a hideous clatter! The robbers, who had already been alarmed by the noisy performance, thought some terrible goblin must be after them, and they all took to their heels and fled into the woods.

Once the coast was clear, the four friends sat down at the table and finished the robbers' splendid meal, feasting as if they hadn't seen food for a month.

When they had finished their meal, they put out the lights and each found a place to sleep. The donkey lay down outside in the yard on a pile of straw; the dog stretched out on a mat behind the front door; the cat curled up on the hearth in front of the ashes of the fire; and the rooster settled himself down on a beam in the ceiling. They soon fell asleep, as they were very tired from their long journey.

As midnight drew near, the robbers, who were watching from afar, saw that no light was burning in their cottage. As it all seemed quiet and still, they thought that maybe they had been in too much of a hurry to run away. The captain, worried that they'd left their lair for no reason, instructed one of the thieves to go back to the cottage and investigate.

The robber crept up to the cottage and peered in the windows. Seeing nothing inside and finding that everything was quiet, he made his way into the dark kitchen. The robber groped around in the dark, trying to find a match so he could light a candle. Hearing a noise, the cat, who had been sleeping in front of the fireplace, woke up and opened her eyes.

The robber spied the glittering eyes of the cat, but he mistook them for burning coals in the fireplace. He stumbled forward, holding out the match to try and light it with the coals, but he only succeeded in poking the poor cat in the face. At once, the cat flew into a rage and jumped up, spitting and scratching the unfortunate robber in the face with her claws.

The frightened robber cried out in terror and ran to the front door, but he stumbled over the dog, who was woken by all the noise. At once, the dog jumped up, growling furiously and biting the robber's ankles and legs with his sharp teeth.

The ill-fated robber ran out the door into the yard, bumping into the donkey, who had got up to investigate what all the fuss was about. The donkey kicked out at the robber with his hind legs, catching the fellow squarely in his chest.

All this time, the rooster, who had also been awoken by the noise, stood in the rafters, crowing out 'Cock-a-doodle-doo!' at the top of his voice.

The robber ran back to his gang as fast as he could to make his report to the captain.

'It was awful!' the robber cried. 'I went into the kitchen, where I was attacked by a horrid witch who spat and scratched at me with her long sharp fingernails!'

The robber paused for breath before continuing.

'As I ran out of the house, I was attacked by a man standing behind the door who stabbed me in my leg with a sharp knife!' he said.

He paused to show his colleagues his bleeding leg.

'Then I fled out into the yard,' said the robber, 'where I ran into a huge black monster, who rose up in front of me and struck me with his huge, heavy club!'

The other gang members gasped as they looked at the robber's bruises.

'Finally, as I ran away, a devil cried out from the roof of the house. "Throw that rascal up to me!" it shrieked. I ran away as fast as I could and I'm never going back there!' the frightened robber finished.

From that time on, the robbers never dared to go back to the house. The four travellers were so pleased with their new quarters that they set up house there and never made it to Bremen. And there they are, it is said, until this very day.

BEAUTY
AND THE
BEAST

There was once a rich merchant who had three sons and three daughters. He spared no expense to give his children the best of everything. His daughters were beautiful, but the youngest was the loveliest. Everyone called her 'Beauty', which made her sisters very jealous.

The two oldest sisters were very proud and refused many offers of marriage because they were waiting for a duke or an earl to ask them. Beauty also refused several offers of marriage, saying she was too young and wished to stay with her father.

Then one day tragedy struck. The merchant's fine house burned down, with all their possessions. Then he discovered that his agents in distant countries had been cheating him out of his earnings. Finally, a great storm wiped out his fleet of ships, which were carrying the last of his goods to market. The merchant's fortune was destroyed.

All that was left was a small house in the country in the middle of a dark forest. The merchant told his children that they must move there and work for their living. The two eldest daughters thought that their fine friends in the city would take them in, but these friends forsook them in their poverty.

When they came to the house, the merchant and his sons worked the land to support them. Beauty rose at four every morning and worked, cooking, spinning and cleaning. She grew stronger and more beautiful than ever and remained cheerful for her father.

But her two sisters rose at ten and spent the day lamenting the loss of their fine clothes and friends. 'Look at our sister,' they said. 'She's such a stupid creature that she's happy with our dismal situation.'

The family had been living there for a year when the merchant received a letter. One of his ships with a rich cargo, which he had thought lost in the storm, had arrived safely to port.

The two oldest sisters were convinced that their poverty was over. They begged their father to bring back new gowns, jewels, ribbons and other trifles. The merchant begged them to be prudent, as he wasn't sure if this cargo was enough to discharge his debts, let alone set up a new fortune. Beauty alone asked for nothing. Her father, noticing her silence, asked her, 'And what shall I bring you, Beauty?'

'I only wish for your safe return, father,' she replied.

Her father was pleased but told her that she should have some pretty present and she should choose something.

'Dear father, if you insist, bring me a rose,' replied Beauty. 'I have not seen one since we arrived here and I love them so much.'

The good merchant set out to town, but when he arrived, it was as he'd feared. After a great deal of trouble, the merchant was left with little more than he had started with. He made his way home, thinking how much he wished to see his children again.

The merchant was still several hours from home as he made his way through a forest. As it grew dark, the wind howled and it started snowing heavily. The merchant realised that he was lost. He heard wolves howling and his clothes were soaked through. Suddenly, he saw a light gleaming through some trees.

As he made his way down a rough track towards the light, the merchant realised that the road was becoming easier. He came out of the forest into an avenue of trees ending at a splendid, illuminated castle.

The merchant made his way to the castle courtyard, but he was surprised to see no one about. However, he saw the stable door was open and went in, finding hay and oats laid out for his horse. The merchant went up to the castle door and entered. He walked through several splendid rooms before he found himself in a large hall with a good fire and a table set out with a feast for one person. He sat in front of the fire to warm himself and waited for the master of the house or some servants to appear, and he soon fell asleep.

The merchant woke when the clock struck eleven but still no one had come. Unable to contain his awful hunger, the merchant ate until he could eat no more. Growing braver, he made his way through more rooms until he found a chamber with a magnificent bed in it. Exhausted, he shut the door and went to sleep.

The next morning, the merchant awoke and discovered a suit of clothes laid out for him. 'Certainly, this place must belong to some fairy,' he thought, amazed.

The merchant looked out the window and saw the most beautiful gardens filled with lovely flowers, and not a trace of snow to be seen. He returned to the great hall and found breakfast laid out.

'Thank you, good fairy,' he said aloud, and then ate his breakfast.

After he had eaten, the merchant made his way outside to find the stables, but passing a rose arbour, he remembered Beauty's request. He gathered one to take to her, but then he heard an awful noise behind him. When the merchant turned around, he saw a frightful beast coming towards him and he fell to his knees.

'Ungrateful wretch!' said the Beast in a terrible voice. 'I saved your life, fed you and warmed you, and you repay me by stealing my roses, which I value above anything else in the world! You shall die for it!'

The merchant cried, 'Oh, please forgive me noble sir! I had no intention to offend. I was gathering a rose to take to my daughter, who asked me to bring her one.'

'Save your flattery!' growled the Beast. 'I am a beast, and I despise compliments!'

In despair, the merchant told the Beast of his misfortunes, why he was travelling in the forest and how Beauty had requested a rose.

The Beast listened, and then said, 'I will forgive you on one condition. You will give me one of your daughters. She must come here willingly. If one of them is brave and loves you enough, it will save your life. I will give you a month to see if any of them will return here. If not, you must come back here. And don't think you can hide, for I shall fetch you.'

The merchant reluctantly agreed. The Beast told him he must stay another night before he could leave. He did as the Beast instructed and found a meal prepared for him in the hall. The next morning, the merchant found another suit laid out for him. He breakfasted, then found his horse in the stables.

The merchant made his way home, where he was greeted by his children, who first thought his errand was a success due to his fine clothes. He handed Beauty her rose, saying to her, 'Here is your rose, although little do you know what it cost me.'

The children listened as their father told them what had happened and the two oldest daughters burst out crying. Beauty did not cry at all and the two sisters angrily accused her of causing their father's death.

'Why, our father will not suffer on my account,' replied Beauty. 'I caused the mischief, and since the Beast will accept one of his daughters, I will offer myself to him in our father's place.'

'Nay,' said the three brothers.

'We kill the monster,

or perish.'

'Do not imagine you could do this,' replied their father. 'The Beast is strong. I am charmed by Beauty's offer but I will not allow it. I am old and have lived my life. I will go.'

'Then I shall follow you and take your place,' insisted Beauty. There was nothing anyone could say to persuade her otherwise.

When the day arrived for her to go, she said goodbye to her brothers and sisters, but she did not cry. She and her father rode to the Beast's castle in the forest. Her father still tried to persuade her to return home but it was in vain.

When they arrived, the castle was lit up as before. In spite of her fear, Beauty could not help but admire the wonderful palace. They made their way into the great hall, where a feast for two awaited them. When they had finished eating, they heard a great roaring and then the Beast entered the hall. Beauty was terrified by his awful appearance but tried to hide it. When the Beast asked her if she had come willingly, she bravely replied, 'Yes.'

'I am pleased,' replied the Beast. Turning to the merchant, he said, 'You must leave at sunrise. Remember, you must never come here again.'

Turning to Beauty, the Beast said, 'Take your father into the next room and choose anything you wish for your father to take with him.'

Beauty and her father found two empty chests. The room was full of splendid dresses, ornaments, jewels and gold. The more they put in the chests, the more room there seemed to be, and they filled them so full that it seemed they'd need an elephant to carry them.

Beauty and her father then went to sleep and Beauty had a vivid dream. She saw a fine lady, who came to her and said, 'What you are doing will not go unrewarded. Be brave.' When Beauty awoke, she told her father the dream and it comforted him a little.

When the time came for the merchant to leave, they found two fine horses waiting in the courtyard carrying the heavy chests. Beauty did not cry until her father rode away. Then she sat in the great hall and wept, as she was sure the Beast would soon eat her.

Beauty decided to take a walk around the castle, as it was very fine. As she walked, she came to a door with 'Beauty's apartment' written above it. When she opened it, she was amazed to see how magnificent it was. She was especially delighted to see a large library, a harpsichord and some music books. 'Surely this preparation would not have been necessary if I were to be eaten,' Beauty thought to herself, and she grew less fearful.

Beauty opened a book and on the first page, she read:

Welcome Beauty, do not fear, you are mistress of all here.

Speak your wishes, state your will, swift obedience meets them still.

'Alas,' sighed Beauty, 'all I want is to see my poor father.'

As soon as she spoke, a great mirror on the wall showed Beauty her father being met by her brothers and sisters. Her brothers looked sorrowful but her sisters could not contain their glee at the chests of treasure. The picture faded after a moment.

That night, as Beauty was sitting down to supper, she heard the Beast approaching. She was terrified, but the Beast asked, 'Will you allow me to join you for dinner?'

'As you please,' answered Beauty. Then the Beast asked her how she had spent her time and she told him about the rooms she found. When the Beast got up to leave after they had eaten, Beauty was surprised that an hour had passed. Maybe the Beast was not as terrible as she had supposed.

As he rose, the Beast asked, 'Beauty, will you marry me?'

Beauty was terrified she would anger him by refusing, but she answered, 'No, Beast.'

The Beast sighed and turned away, saying, 'Then good night Beauty.'

Welcome Beauty,
do not fear,
you are mistress
of all here.
Speak your wishes,
state your will,
swift obedience
meets them still.

When he had left, Beauty felt very sorry for the Beast. 'It is such a pity that someone so good natured should be so ugly.'

Beauty spent many months at the palace. Every day she found new surprises at the castle and every evening the Beast joined her for dinner and they talked for hours. Beauty got used to him and looked forward to his visits more than any other part of her day. She found the Beast was exceedingly kind and good-natured. The only worry was that every night as he left the table, the Beast asked her to marry him.

One day she said to him, 'Beast, I wish I could consent to marry you, as I see how my refusal saddens you. However, I am too sincere to make you think that might happen, but I love you as my greatest friend. Can you endeavour to be happy with that?'

'Alas, I love you with all my heart,' answered the Beast, 'but I must be happy with that, if you will promise to stay here always. Can you promise me that?'

Beauty hesitated, for that day in the mirror, she had seen her father, deathly ill from grief at her loss. 'I could promise, but I have such a desire to see my poor father that I might die if I can't,' she said.

'I would rather die myself than see you unhappy,' said the Beast. 'I will return you to your father and you will remain there and I shall die from grief.'

'No!' cried Beauty and she started to weep. 'I love you too much to be the cause of your death. Let me see my father for a month and then I shall return and stay with you forever!'

'You will be there tomorrow,' the Beast told her, 'but remember your promise. Take this ring. When it is time to return, twist it on your finger and say, "I wish to go back to my palace and see my Beast again." Sleep well Beauty and you shall soon see your father again.'

The next morning, Beauty awoke to find she was in a room in her father's house, along with a trunk filled with her clothes. She rushed to greet her father and her brothers and sisters. They were amazed to see her and asked her many questions. When they heard she was only there for a month, they lamented loudly.

As the month passed, Beauty found that nothing amused her and she found herself thinking of the palace and the Beast. When the month was over, her brothers begged her to stay a few days longer, as their father was recovering his health every day. Beauty missed the Beast, but she did not have the courage to say goodbye to her family just yet, and so, day after day, she put off her departure.

One night, she had a dream. She was wandering along a path in the palace gardens when she heard groans coming from behind some bushes. Pushing them apart, she found a cave entrance. Inside, she found the Beast stretched out on his side, dying. The fine lady from her first dream appeared and said to her, 'You are only just in time to save his life. This is what happens if people do not keep their promises!'

Beauty awoke in fright and discovered it was morning. She ran to her family and told them she must go back. That night, she said goodbye to her father and then twisted the ring on her finger, saying, 'I wish to go back to my palace and see my Beast again.' She immediately fell asleep. When she awoke the next day, she discovered she was back in her room in the palace.

Beauty put on one of her finest dresses and waited for dinner to see the Beast. But dinner time came and went and there was no sign of him. After waiting a long time, she ran through the palace trying to find him. She ran into the garden, looking for him, until she came to a path that she recognised from her dream.

Sure enough, behind some bushes was the cave, and stretched out on the ground was the Beast. Beauty ran to him and stroked his head, but he did not move or open his eyes. Crying, she ran to a fountain and fetched some water. When she sprinkled it on his head, the Beast opened his eyes.

'Oh, how you have frightened me!' she wept. 'I never knew how much I loved you until now, when I thought it was too late to tell you!'

'Can you really love something as ugly as me?' asked the Beast. 'Ah Beauty, I was dying because I thought you had forgotten me. Go to the palace and wait for me there.'

Beauty returned to the hall. The Beast came to her and sat with her to eat dinner. They talked about her visit to her family. When dinner was over, the Beast rose to leave, and then asked her, 'Beauty, will you marry me?'

'Yes, dear Beast,' she answered.

As she spoke, a blaze of light erupted outside. It seemed that fireworks were exploding outside and triumphant music was playing. Turning to the Beast to ask him what all this meant, she saw that the Beast had disappeared and in his place stood a handsome prince.

When she asked where the Beast was, the prince replied, 'You see him here. An evil witch cursed me to remain a beast until a beautiful maiden agreed to marry me without knowing who I really was. Only you were able love me for my goodness underneath my ugly form and I love you with all my heart.'

Then Beauty and the prince were transported to the prince's kingdom, where they were greeted by two stately ladies. Beauty recognised one from her dreams and the other was so grand that she must be the queen. The lady from her dreams, who was a good fairy, said, 'Queen, this is Beauty, who had the courage to rescue your son from his curse. Only your consent to their marriage is needed to make them perfectly happy.'

'I consent with all my heart!' cried the queen, and she embraced her son and Beauty. The fairy sent for Beauty's family and they joyfully arrived for the wedding, which was celebrated with the utmost splendour. Even her sisters were happy for Beauty and they all lived happily ever after.

THE END

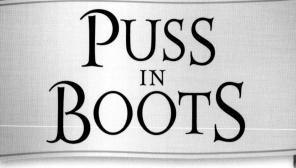

PUSS IN BOOTS

The best-known version of *Puss in Boots* was written by Frenchman Charles Perrault in 1697. It was included in *Contes de ma Mère l'Oye (Tales of my Mother Goose)*, a collection of fairytales and stories.

It is thought that Perrault adapted his story from the earliest known recorded version of the tale called *Fortunato Costantino*. This was written by an Italian, Giovanni Francesco Straparola, in the 1550s, who included it in his collection of stories, *The Facetious Nights of Straparola*. Another Italian, Giambattista Basile, included a version called *Caglioso* in the collection *Il Pentamerone* in the 1630s.

There are many variants of the *Puss in Boots* story that can be found in different cultures around the world. The cat is not always male in these stories: sometimes she is female. Animals other than cats are also used in the helper role, such as a fox or a gazelle. In some versions, the cat is actually a fairy in disguise or a woman who has been bewitched, who ends up marrying her master once the spell has been removed.

Another common variation has the cat testing its owner's gratitude by pretending to be dead or dangerously ill. The owner promises the cat a burial in a golden coffin when it dies. However, when the owner refuses to provide treatment for the sick cat or orders the supposedly dead cat's body be thrown on a dung heap or down a well, the cat either angrily takes its leave or reveals the humble origins of its owner. Perrault opted for a much happier ending for his cat, living out a life of leisure and amusement.

THE LITTLE MERMAID

Written by Hans Christian Andersen in 1836, *The Little Mermaid* was first published in a collection called *Fairy Tales, Told for Children* in 1837. The story remains hugely popular, with adaptations created for theatre, ballet and film.

Hans Christian Andersen originally created the story with a much sadder ending, with the little mermaid dissolving away into foam. However, Andersen claimed that the working title of the story was 'The Daughter of Air' and that the ending where the little mermaid is transformed was intended from the start. This gives the little mermaid more control over her own destiny, instead of relying on the love of another.

Andersen later revised the ending to make it more moralistic. In the final version, whenever a child is good, a year is taken off the 300 years that the daughters of air must wait to receive their immortal soul. However, children's bad behaviour makes the daughters of air cry, which adds a day to their wait for every tear shed.

The story of *The Little Mermaid* is so popular that a small statute of the mermaid perched on a rock in Copenhagen harbour is one of Denmark's major tourist attractions.

THE VALIANT TAILOR

*T*he *Valiant Tailor* was published by the Brothers Grimm in the 1812 first edition of their collection of fairytales, *Kinder- und Hausmärchen (Children's and Household Tales)*. The story was revised in later editions into the version known today.

In their notes for the tale, the Grimm Brothers point out the many different versions of this tale that they found throughout Europe. The story's two parts can stand alone as individual tales, with the tailor's encounter with the giant the first and his three tasks the second.

The Grimms note that the first section is taken in part from an Austrian story where a tailor enters the service of a giant. The second part was taken from a collection of stories called *Wegkürzer* by Martinus Montanus. However, variations on the second part can be found in stories from all over Europe, and as far afield as Persia. The profession of the tailor in these stories is sometimes changed to a cobbler.

The Grimm Brothers also note that the nature of the tailor's adventures with the giants vary in these stories. In one tale, the belt is replaced by a shield. The number of flies killed ranges from five to 500. The tasks the tailor performs also include killing a bear, defeating an army and overcoming two magicians. Whatever the variation, the tailor triumphs over his low origins through quick thinking, a sharp mind and his bravery, outwitting fearsome giants and royalty in the process.

ALADDIN

*A*laddin was originally published in the collection *1001 Arabian Nights*, which was translated from Arabic into French by Antoine Galland. However, the story of *Aladdin* never appeared in the original Arabic manuscript but was actually added by Galland in 1710.

Galland claims to have heard the original version of *Aladdin* from a storyteller named Hanna Diab from the city of Aleppo in Syria, who was visiting Paris in 1705. Early Arabic manuscripts of *Aladdin* have been found, however one was written after Galland's translation and the other is a copy of a lost earlier version.

The original story of *Aladdin* is set in China, despite the fact that the customs, names and titles of the rulers are very definitely Arabic. The sorcerer is from the Maghreb, a region of North Africa that includes Morocco, Tunisia and Algeria. At one time, these two regions would have been at the ends of the known world, emphasising how far the sorcerer travels to find the lamp and how far away he transports the Princess.

The word genie comes from an Arabic word: *jinni*. Also called djinn or jinn, genies were thought to be spirits made of smokeless fire. The term *jinni* comes from a word meaning hidden from sight or concealed. Genies have the power to fly and move from place to place very quickly. They can also fit into any space, large or small.

TOM THUMB

The Brothers Grimm recorded two stories featuring the original *Tom Thumb* character: *Thumbling* and *Thumbling's Travels*. The version presented in this collection is the original *Thumbling*.

In the sequel, *Thumbling's Travels*, Tom (or Thumbling) is carried up the chimney by the steam from the pot. He helps some robbers steal from the king's treasure chamber, is cooked into a black pudding and eventually eaten by a fox, who he convinces to let him go and rides back home. His father is so grateful that he allows the fox to eat his chickens.

It is thought that the folktale that the Brothers Grimm based their version on was the precursor to an English folktale of the same name. The English version combines the events of the two *Thumbling* stories and also mixes in many elements and characters of the King Arthur legends.

In the English version, the magician Merlin, disguised as a peasant, is given shelter by a childless couple. Out of gratitude, he casts a spell so that Tom Thumb is born. Tom ends up having many adventures, including a visit to fairyland, and he becomes an honorary Knight of the Round Table.

This story was recorded in verse by Richard Johnson in 1621. It was turned into a popular satirical play by the playwright Henry Fielding in 1730.

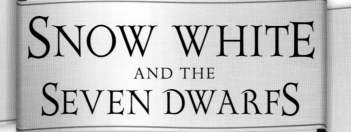

SNOW WHITE
AND THE
SEVEN DWARFS

The story of *Snow White* was told in many versions from Europe to Asia and Africa before the Brothers Grimm recorded it in *Kinder- und Hausmärchen (Children's and Household Tales)*.

Some traditional versions of the story have Snow White rescued by robbers instead of dwarfs. Instead of a magic mirror, the step-mother converses with the sun or moon, or sometimes an animal.

Although it was included in the 1810 manuscript of their collection, the Brothers Grimm changed *Snow White* quite dramatically in the published edition. Initially, it was Snow White's own mother who tried to kill her, not her step-mother. Her mother takes her into the woods to gather flowers, then abandons her. At the end of the story, the king has his wife executed. It is thought this was changed by the Brothers Grimm to make the story more suitable for children.

In the final version of the Grimms' story, the evil step-mother eats the heart the hunter gives her as proof of Snow White's death. She also attends the wedding, where the prince forces her to dance wearing red-hot iron shoes until she falls down dead. Modern versions of the story have Snow White awakened with a kiss, instead of the apple jolting free from her mouth.

THE MUSICIANS OF BREMEN

The Brothers Grimm recorded *The Musicians of Bremen* in *Kinder- und Hausmärchen (Children's and Household Tales)*. It is the twenty-seventh story in their collection and was first included in the second edition, which was published in 1819.

In their introduction to the tale, the Brothers Grimm note that they found several versions of the story, including one in which the musicians don't drive out the robbers but peacefully join them for a meal and then entertain them. It is when the gang returns from thieving that they think they are being attacked, like in the Grimms' version.

The harbour town of Bremen is in northern Germany near the coast on the river Weser. In the story, the animals decide to head for Bremen because it is 'renowned for its freedom'. Bremen was a member city of the Hanseatic League, a wealthy trading guild that operated in the Baltic Sea. Towns of the League had no local nobles or aristocracy and owed their allegiance directly to the Holy Roman Emperor. Cities in the League could be found along the coast from France to Estonia.

Although the animals never made it to Bremen, there is a famous statue of the four friends perched on each other's backs in the town.

BEAUTY AND THE BEAST

Versions of the *Beauty and the Beast* story have been told for centuries. An ancient Roman myth called *Cupid and Psyche* features a beautiful maiden cursed by the goddess Venus to fall in love with a snake. However, Venus's son Cupid falls in love with Psyche and turns himself into the serpent, revealing himself as a young man at the end of the tale. The story of a beautiful girl caring for a beast, only to have him turn into a man, is found throughout many tales from Asia and Europe.

Other early European versions of the story include *The Pig King* by Italian Giovanni Straparola, published in *The Facetious Nights of Straparola* in 1550 with the beast as a pig, and the first version to be named *Beauty and the Beast*, written in 1650 by French aristocrat Marie-Catherine Le Jumel de Barneville and featuring a serpent beast.

In 1740, Madame Gabrielle-Suzanne Barbot de Gallon de Villeneuve wrote the first modern version of the tale. Her version of *Beauty and the Beast* was 362 pages long and featured fairies, kings and twelve brothers and sisters.

The version of *Beauty and the Beast* most familiar to modern readers was published 1756 by Madame Jeanne-Marie Le Prince de Beaumont, in a collection called *Magasin des enfants*. This version has the two jealous sisters marrying wealthy men, only to have unhappy marriages, while Beauty, who accepts the hideous but good Beast, ends up happy and content.

ILLUSTRATORS

MELISSA WEBB

The Little Mermaid

Beauty and the Beast

ANTON PETROV

WATERMARK - AUCKLAND STUDIO

Puss in Boots

SUZIE BYRNE

The Musicians of Bremen

OMAR ARANDA

NICK DIGGORY ILLUSTRATION

The Valiant Tailor

Tom Thumb

DEAN JONES

Snow White
and the Seven Dwarfs

MIRELA TUFAN

Aladdin